BiG

Daniel Kirk

G.P. PUTNAM'S SONS ● NEW YORK

This book
is for Raleigh,
my **BIG** boy.

Once I was very small.
I was so small that
I was hardly even me.

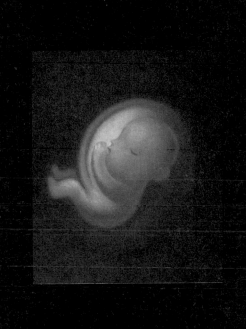

But every day, in the
darkness of my mother's
womb, I grew. I grew
bigger, and bigger,
and bigger, until . . .

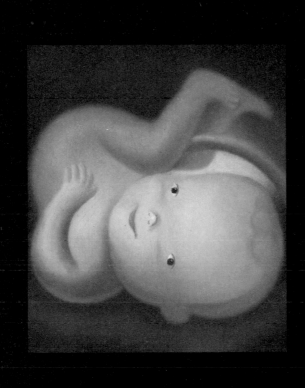

I was born! I pushed hard with my little arms and kicked hard with my little legs, and guess what?

I got bigger. I kept growing
when the sun shone,
and by the light of the moon.

Even though I did not know how to walk, or talk, or dress or feed myself, there was always one thing I knew how to do — grow!

Nothing could stop me now,
because I was getting bigger.
"My, how you've grown,"
people would say. "What a big
boy you are!" And I knew
they were right.

They were right, because
when I stood next to the table,
I could see what was on top of
it instead of just underneath.
I could stand on my toes and
touch the doorknob, and the
telephone, and the light switch
on the wall . . . even though
I wasn't supposed to.

Boxes were filled with my old shirts and coats and pants and shoes, because they did not fit me anymore. Only big clothes would fit me now!

I took big steps, ate big meals, and used big words.
I slept in a big bed and went to a big school.
I played with big toys and bigger boys!

Sometimes I didn't
like it when other kids
played with my toys.
But I was getting bigger—
big enough to share.
And as I got bigger,
my world began to grow.

I learned the names
of animals I had never
seen, and then I went
to see them.

I saw the houses all around my own, and the people who lived in them. I learned their names, and they learned mine.

I learned about the oceans, and the mountains, and the stars in the sky, a million miles away.

Everywhere I looked, I saw my world getting bigger, and everything I saw I took inside, and I was big enough to hold it all.

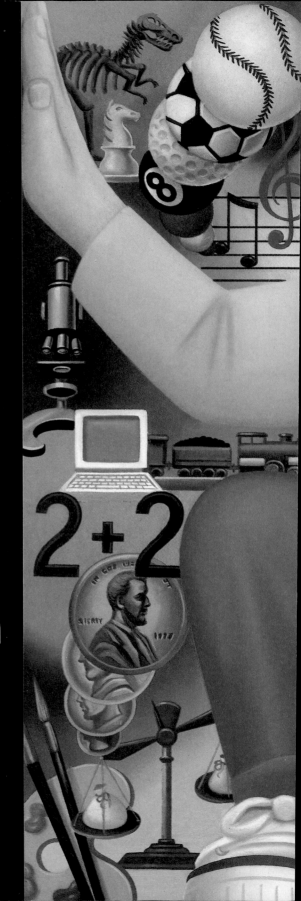

Once I was very small.
I was so small that I
was hardly even me. But
there in the darkness,
before I knew my own
name, before I ever
saw my mother's smiling
face or held my father's
hand, was a promise.
It was the promise of
everything that I am,
and everything that I
will be, as I grow bigger
and bigger and
bigger!